LOADING

ALSO BY CHRIS BRADFORD

Gamer (Virtual Kombat 1)
Virus (Virtual Kombat 2)

Bulletcatcher
Bulletcatcher: Blowback
Bulletcatcher: Sniper

S.P.E.A.R. (Bulletcatcher omnibus)

Ninja: First Mission
Ninja: Death Touch
Ninja: Assassin

Shadow Warriors (Ninja omnibus)

CYBORG

CHRIS BRADFORD

With illustrations by
ANDERS FRANG

Barrington Stoke

**To David,
A true brother in arms!**

**For more information on Chris and his books
visit: www.chrisbradford.co.uk**

First published in 2019 in Great Britain by
Barrington Stoke Ltd
18 Walker Street, Edinburgh, EH3 7LP

www.barringtonstoke.co.uk

Text © 2019 Chris Bradford
Illustrations © 2019 Anders Frang

A CIP catalogue record for this book is available
from the British Library upon request

ISBN: 978-1-78112-708-7

Printed in China by Leo

CONTENTS

Virtual Kombat is the most realistic fighting game ever. Choose your avatar and enter the VK battle arenas — where every enemy has a mind of its own. Feel the thrill ... *and* the pain of every fight!

THE ULTIMATE PRIZE!

Win the VK Crown and get ten million credits and your name in the Warrior Hall of Fame!

Are You An Elite Gamer?

KOMBAT

SO REAL IT HURTS

Watch out for the VK Selector Truck in *your* zone.

Jump into a PlayPod, play the game and prove your skills to win your place at Vince Power's Home for Elite Gamers!

WATCH VK LIVE

THE NO. 1 ENTERTAINMENT SHOW ON THE PLANET!

VIRUS

UPDATE v2.1

This update provides key data and compatibility improvements for new and returning gamers:

- In the year 2030, a killer virus wiped out millions of adults and left a generation of orphans on the streets.

- Adult survivors stayed indoors and escaped into a life on the internet.

- Virtual Kombat became the #1 game on the web and was credited with cutting violent crime and restoring law and order around the world.

- VK inventor and multi-billionaire Vince Power set up his City Orphanage for Elite Gamers in 2032.

- The VK Selector Truck began testing thousands of children and choosing Elite Gamers – saving them from starvation on the streets.

- Scott was selected and trained as an Elite Gamer, but he soon discovered VK was *more* than just a game.

- Targeted for termination, Scott escaped and went on the run.

- Hunted by Wasp drones, Scott was saved by a girl called Java, a member of a secret rebel group, the VKR – Virtual Kombat Rebellion.

- Scott joined the VKR to help in its mission to hack into VK and bring down the game from within.

- Risking their lives, they implanted a virus in the game's code.

- Virtual Kombat was destroyed, but Scott is about to discover the game is not yet over …

For a full update, read GAMER and VIRUS, #1 and #2 in the Virtual Kombat series.

My opponent's fist comes shooting at me like a bullet. I duck to the left. She aims a roundhouse-kick at my head. I lean back and her foot misses me by a fraction. Her eyes narrow as she fires more punches at me. I block a back-fist ... counter her attack with an elbow-strike ... duck under a hook-punch ... then go for a body blow. But she moves too fast for me to land a hit.

We fight our way down a martial arts hall – an old concrete building that's lit by red Chinese lanterns. Deadly weapons decorate the wall, a battered punchbag hangs from the ceiling and a wooden training dummy sits in

the far corner. Outside, the cold neon
displays of the Street Screens
flicker like distant lightning.

I go to sweep my opponent
off her feet but she catches me in
the jaw with an upper-cut first. Stars burst
in front of my eyes and I'm forced to retreat.
More strikes pummel me – I need to end this
fight before she ends me!

So I jump into the air for my most lethal
move: a spinning hook-kick. But I mis-time the
leap. My legs get tangled and I crash-land onto
my back. My head hits the wooden floor and I
black out—

"Is he alive?" asks a voice from far away.

I blink and my opponent's face swims
into focus – Java, with a stripe of black
make-up across her half-moon eyes. "He's

moving at least," she says. She sounds almost disappointed.

Spam gives me a chubby grin, his blue eyes twinkling behind his round glasses. "Welcome back, Scott! Enjoy your nap?" he jokes.

My mind is dazed. My head's throbbing. I can taste blood in my mouth. But I know the pain will soon go. It's just an after-effect of the virtual world I was fighting in. The game of VK is so lifelike that the brain is fooled for a moment, believing the injuries are real.

Pac-Man holds out a hand to help me up. His muscles ripple under his T-shirt. Then Cookie examines my head, her fringe of brown hair partly hiding her slim dark face. That's when I realise I'm *not* in a PlayPod. I *wasn't* plugged into a virtual world. The fight was real. The blood is real. And the pain in my head is real!

Java sees the shock on my face and laughs. "We're not in VK any more," she says. "You *can't* do flying-kicks like that!"

Groaning, I rub my bruised skull. "Well, I won't be trying that move again!" I say.

"Don't fear failure," a soft voice croaks. "In great attempts, it is glorious even to fall."

I look over to an old man who is sitting on a small wooden stool. His face is lined like the bark of a tree. He wears a simple black cotton shirt and trousers, and his feet are bare. His name is Sifu – our martial arts teacher.

A fly buzzes by my ear and I wave it away. "I could do that kick easily in Virtual Kombat," I tell him, "but I guess it's impossible in the real world."

"Is it?" says Sifu, rising from his stool. He leaps up, spins in mid-air and hook-kicks the punchbag.

We all stare in amazement at the old man. Sifu doesn't look like he could run for an Auto-Bus, but he just flew like a Wasp drone!

"How did you do that?" I gasp.

"Practice," our teacher says with a smile. He hobbles over.

I can recall the first time we met Sifu, a month after VK Day – the day we defeated Vince Power and took his deadly VK video game offline with a computer virus. We'd been given the address to an old martial arts hall but were having trouble finding it. As we searched the back streets, Cookie spotted an elderly man punching a wooden post over and over again. We thought he needed help, so stopped to ask what the problem was. The old man just smiled and replied that his problem was now solved. He led us into the martial arts hall we'd been looking for and our training began.

Three months later, Sifu still hasn't explained why he was punching the post – and we are still his *only* students.

Sifu shuffles to a stop beside me. "Practice is everything," he instructs. "Fear not the man who has practised 10,000 kicks once. Fear the man who has practised one kick 10,000 times!"

"Sounds like a lot of hard work to me!" says Spam, who prefers to watch the sessions rather than train. "Why learn martial arts anyway? You can master it online in seconds!"

Sifu tuts and gives Spam a hard look. "True martial arts is a lifelong journey, not an instant download!"

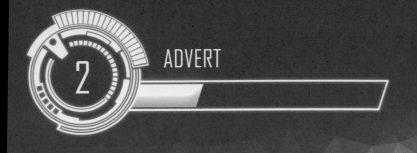
After our training session, I stumble out of the
martial arts hall and into the street, which is
wet with acid rain. Java limps alongside me,
her leg still hurting after Pac-Man kicked her
too hard in the final bout.

"I don't know why you punish yourselves
like that," Spam says as we head home. His
gaze is fixed on his mobile gaming console,
playing Speed Racer. "Fighting is far safer and
less painful in a virtual arena!"

"It wasn't safe when VK was burning
gamers out!" Pac-Man replies, his eye swollen

from where Java elbowed him. "I'd prefer a black eye to a burned-out brain any day!"

Cookie puts on her grey jacket against the rain, saying, "Pentium told us to detox, remember, Spam?" With a guilty look, Spam switches off the console and slips it in his pocket.

Pentium is Vince Power's twin brother and the true brain behind VK. After Vince tried to burn Pentium out, leaving him in a wheelchair, Pentium recruited us to hack into VK and shut it down from within. But a side effect of being an Elite Gamer is memory loss. Spend too much time in the virtual world and you begin to forget your real self. So Pentium ordered us to limit our virtual-reality time and exercise more. He recommended Sifu's martial arts classes as the perfect remedy.

Sifu is an old friend of Pentium's. He's never been into gaming, but Pentium told us Sifu was the inspiration for many of the trademark moves that he'd programmed into VK. Like the others, I'd been curious to meet this legend and learn his martial arts. But for me the training means more than a digital detox. It reminds me of my father. Before he'd died in the killer virus of 2030, my dad had taught me *tae kwon do*, the Korean martial art. Those fighting skills were the reason I survived on the streets and became one of the best gamers in VK.

"There may be no Burn Outs any more," Java mumbles. "But it's been four months since VK Day and nothing's *really* changed. What did we risk our lives for?"

She gazes up at the countless 3D Street Screens. They shine above our heads like alien suns in the smog. Many of the screens are advertising the newest hit video game: VIRTUA.

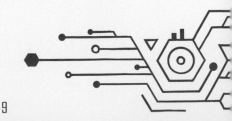

Build your own world!
Own and sell virtual land!
Live Rich! Live Fast! Live VIRTUA!

"Violence has just been replaced with greed!"
Java says, and shakes her head. "I thought we'd
make a difference!"

"We did!" Cookie argues. "Like you said,
there are no Burn Outs any more. Kids aren't
brain dead or dying."

"But where did all the Elite Gamers go?"
Spam asks.

I shrug. "It's a big city," I reply.

In fact, the mega-city is so vast, a million
people could be added and no one would notice.
But that doesn't explain why all the PlayPods
in Vince Power's warehouse were empty when
VK went offline. It was as if the Elite Gamers
had become ghosts. So far we've found only a

few wandering the streets and they'd lost their memories after so long in the game.

As my friends discuss the Elite Gamers' disappearance, a burst of static fills my ears. I turn towards an old tech shop. In the window, a TV screen flickers to life. A grinning face leers out at me with perfect white teeth and a mane of silver hair.

"Playtime, Scott!" he says, the voice familiar and as smooth as silk.

My mouth drops open and I stare, horrified, at the ghostly image of Vince Power.

"It's no longer just a game!" he tells me, laughing. Then the VK red and black logo flashes on the screen.

Panicking, I call to my friends, "Do you see this?"

They stop and turn. "See what?" Cookie asks.

I point at the screen. "Vince Power! He just spoke to me!"

They all look at the shop window and frown. An advert for a Zing energy bar is playing.

"Maybe you hit your head a bit *too* hard, Scott?" Spam suggests.

"Or else he should have hit it harder!" Java says with a laugh.

Pac-Man slaps me on the back. "Vince is dead, buddy. You're seeing things."

I shake my head. "I know what I saw!"

Cookie holds up her wrist. "You should get Pentium to give you an Ad Blocker implant," she says. "Cuts out all the personal ads from the Street Screens."

My friends walk on. But I stay stuck to the spot and peer closer at the screen. An advert for vita-shakes comes on. I wait for Vince to reappear, the hairs on my neck rising as I get the feeling I'm being watched. I spin round ... but it's just a cleaner droid sweeping the streets. *Spam is right*, I think as the squat, round city-bot hoovers past. *Maybe I did hit my head too hard*. Then a bag is pulled over my eyes and I'm dragged away.

"Blaze him!" a voice growls.

I'm struggling to escape my captors, but I can't see and there are too many of them.

"Dump his body in the garbage!" a girl hisses.

Fear grips me as I'm shoved against a brick wall and my arms are pinned to my sides. Then the bag is ripped off my head and I see a tall, thin boy with slick black hair and a busted nose glaring at me.

My eyes widen. "Stick!" I gasp, recognising my old enemy from the streets. He's surrounded by four other mean-looking kids.

Stick grins at me. "You still have a debt to pay, Scott ... with interest!"

He pulls down the collar of his T-shirt. There's a cobweb of scars on his chest – the burn lines from an electro-dart Stinger fired by a Wasp. The drone had been targeting me but had hit Stick instead.

"I tried to warn you," I remind him.

"Like you warned Juice?" Stick replies with a scowl.

"I didn't kill your friend," I protest. "He fell!"

Stick punches me hard across the jaw. My head rings from the blow and I spit out blood.

"That was for Juice," Stick says. "Now tell me, are you to blame for VK going offline too?"

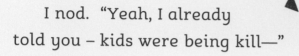

I nod. "Yeah, I already told you – kids were being kill—"

He hits me in the stomach and I double over, gasping for breath.

"So it's *your* fault the VK Selector Trucks have all gone," Stick snarls.

Vince used the trucks to recruit new gamers, bribing them with food packs and testing their gaming skills to win a place at his City Orphanage. But it was a lie. The recruits were simply "fresh meat" for the PlayPods – used until they burned out!

"You don't ... understand ..." I say, gulping in air. "I saved you from—"

Stick knees me between the legs and I drop to the ground. Then his gang start to punch and kick me like a football.

"No more food packs!" Stick shouts. "No way off these dirty streets! You had no right to stop VK!"

He stamps on my back and I lie groaning at his feet. My body's bruised and bleeding.

"Street life is even harder now," Stick says with bitterness. "Less food to go round and more kids than ever!"

I look up at Stick, surprised. "You mean the missing Elite Gamers?"

"Well, they're more like zombies!" he replies. "They just wander around, lost. Too many for *my* turf. So I'm cleaning up the streets. And I'll start with you!" Stick pulls a Blazer from his back pocket and flicks on the red pulse-blade. "This time there are no Wasps to save you."

I scramble away. Stick's gang grab me. But now I can see, I'm able to fight back. I drive one boy into the ground with a shoulder-throw. I elbow another in the face. A third gang member tries to punch me, but I block his fist and knife-hand him in the throat. He stumbles away, choking.

Sifu's martial arts training is paying off!

The girl now rushes forward and claws at my face. I twist her hand into a wristlock. She screams in pain and I force her to the floor. I turn to make my escape, but I'm met by the burning red glow of Stick's Blazer.

"You *will* pay your debt!" he snarls, and thrusts the blade into my gut.

"No!" I cry. But at the last second, the pulse-blade dies. Stick clicks the trigger again. Nothing.

"Out of juice?" a girl's voice teases.

Stick spins round. Java is standing at the end of the alley, an EMP gun in her hand. I realise her Electro-Magnetic Pulse weapon has short-circuited Stick's Blazer. Relief floods over me as I spot Pac-Man, Spam and Cookie with Java too.

Stick spits with rage. With his gang injured and out of action, he gives up the fight and retreats. "You won't always have your friends watching your back!" he yells.

"Training take its toll today?" Pentium asks as I limp into his penthouse office. We're on the top floor of Power Inc., the former headquarters of VK. As the joint creator of the game, Pentium re-took control over the company when Vince died on VK Day.

"Met an old *friend* on the street," I reply.

Pentium glances up from his holo-desk and sees my bruised face. "Not much of a friend by the looks of it!"

He glides round his desk in his motorised wheelchair and heads towards a white glass door. The door slides open and I follow him into the gleaming tech lab. "He wasn't happy that VK went offline," I explain. "Says street life is even harder."

There's a black full-body metal suit standing in the middle of the room, complete with a helmet and visor. Since Pentium took charge at Power Inc., he's been using its resources to design a machine to help him walk again. It's the first time I've seen it and I gasp, asking, "Is this the exo-suit you've been working on?"

Pentium nods and grins. "It's finally ready for its test run!" Then he sighs. "We need to do more to help those kids on the street. I'll set up extra food stations and another three shelters."

"Will that be enough?" I ask as I examine Pentium's bionic suit. I know he's using the vast profits from VK to fund a city-wide relief programme. But it's like putting a sticking plaster over a gaping wound – the problem is simply too big.

"It is never enough," Pentium replies sadly. "But I'm hoping my new video game will bring society together again."

I turn from the suit to Pentium, suddenly interested. "What new game?"

He taps the side of his nose to indicate it's a secret. "It's an augmented-reality game. The real world ... only better!"

"Can't you even give me a clue?" I plead.

"The launch is very soon," Pentium says. "But I promise you'll get first look, Scott." He flashes me a smile that's scarily like his twin brother's and it reminds me of the face I saw on the Street Screen.

"Pentium ... could your brother have survived VK?" I ask.

Pentium blinks, then shakes his head. "Vince was trapped in an Infinity Drop when the program corrupted. He had zero chance of escape."

"But we never found his PlayPod or his body," I point out.

"It doesn't matter," Pentium says. "Vince would've been brain dead anyway. His Analysts most likely cremated him."

I tell Pentium about Vince's message to me.

Pentium frowns. "Strange ... but it may just be a Tetris Effect."

"What's Tetris?" I ask.

"It's an old video game where you matched tiles in a puzzle," Pentium explains. "If people played it for a long time, they'd continue to think about how different shapes could fit together when in the real world, such as bricks

in a wall or boxes on a supermarket shelf. Many gamers dreamed of Tetris. Some even imagined pieces slotting into an invisible grid!"

"So are you saying I imagined Vince?" I ask.

"It's the most likely explanation," Pentium replies. "You went so deep into VK that your brain could've been affected. What you saw was probably a flashback or a glitch."

"A glitch?" I cry. "But Vince spoke *directly* to me."

"Is that why you messaged me about getting an Ad Blocker?" Pentium asks.

I nod. "It's Cookie's idea. But if it's a Tetris Effect, a microchip won't stop it."

"It's worth a try." Pentium presses a call button on his wheelchair. "Ad scanners will pick up your thoughts and select adverts to match. Your brain may have triggered an old

VK ad featuring Vince, which the Tetris Effect altered."

A tech walks in with a slim silver syringe on a tray. He places it on a lab bench, then leaves.

"Are you sure you can do this?" I ask, seeing the tremble in Pentium's hands. Since his partial Burn Out, Pentium no longer has full control over his upper limbs and I'm a bit worried about his medical skills.

"Absolutely," he replies. "I just need some assistance." Pentium nods at the exo-suit. I help him to clamber in. The metal plates close around his body, the helmet slides on and a neon blue line lights up in the visor.

"The suit's self-adjusting," Pentium explains. He winces and adds, "Always a bit of a shock when the neuro-connection goes in the neck. You can let me go now."

I step away and for the first time I see Pentium stand on his own. He looks like a sleek armoured robocop.

"The suit is made of ultra-light bitanium," he says. "An Auto-Bus could run over me and I'd be fine. My nerve impulses are boosted so I can walk, run and even jump. In my wheelchair, I'm as weak as a kitten. In *this*, I'm a superman."

With one hand, Pentium lifts up his electric wheelchair.

My eyes widen. "That's amazing!"

He reaches for a coffee cup on a lab bench and picks it up between his metal-gloved fingers. "See?" Pentium says. "I can be powerful or gentle—" Suddenly the cup explodes in his fist. I duck as pieces fly past and cold coffee splatters everywhere.

Pentium looks sheepish. "Takes a bit of getting used to ... My techs are still fine-tuning the strength settings."

I study the silver syringe on the tray, then reply, "I think I'd better do this myself."

When I walk to Sifu's martial arts hall the
next day, it's as if the volume of the world has
been turned down. The Street Screens still
shine bright in the smog, but I'm no longer
bombarded with personal adverts. It's almost
a pleasure to stroll along the city's gloomy
streets, even in the acid rain. I don't have any
strange visions of Vince and begin to think the
video message must have been the result of the
Tetris Effect.

When I arrive at the hall, I find Sifu
punching his wooden post.

"You're early," Sifu says as his fist leaves tiny dents in the battered wood.

"I wanted to get some extra training in," I reply. "Practise my spinning hook-kick."

My teacher looks at the bruises on my face and nods. No further explanation required. He returns to punching the post.

After an hour of jumping and spinning, I'm still no closer to mastering the kick, but I'm even more curious about Sifu's training. "Why are you always hitting that post?" I ask.

Sifu lines his fist up a short distance from the wood. Then he strikes. Fast and hard. The power in the short punch is immense and cracks the post. Sifu smiles as if he has solved a lifelong problem.

"To learn," he replies.

"Learn what?" I ask.

"Bruce Lee's one-inch punch."

I frown. "Who's Bruce Lee?"

Sifu looks at me and rolls his eyes. "Just the most famous martial artist to have lived, before the killer virus. Bruce Lee's one-inch punch was said to be twice as deadly as a car crash ... and I think I'm *starting* to master it."

I examine the damage to the post and realise the one-inch punch is like a high-level Mod in VK. Such a move would've helped me when I was grabbed by Stick's gang. "Can you teach me?" I ask.

Sifu steps aside and invites me to stand before the wooden post. "The one-inch punch uses *fa jin*," he explains. "Explosive power. A chain reaction of muscle and movement from knee to hip to shoulder to elbow to wrist. The timing is key. A shockwave of energy needs to pass from you to your target."

Sifu demonstrates the punch on me and I go flying. It's as if a high-powered Stinger has hit my chest.

"*Wow!*" I gasp, struggling to get my breath back.

When I'm finally on my feet again, Sifu shows me the technique in slow motion. I copy him, repeating it several times. Then, using all my energy, I drive my fist into the post. There is a loud *crunch*! But it's not the wood – it's my fist. Pain rockets up my arm. "That's impossible!" I moan.

Sifu shakes his head. "You can't hope to grasp such a move in five minutes, or even five years!" he says. "Study Bruce Lee videos in the archives online. Watch. Practise. Learn."

As I nurse my throbbing fist, Sifu shuffles over to a low table. "Come, join me for breakfast."

We sit cross-legged, two bowls of steaming noodles in front of us. Sifu shovels the food into his mouth with chopsticks. But I can barely hold my chopsticks with my sore hand and the noodles slip back into the bowl.

"Bruce Lee's skills are a forgotten art," Sifu says sadly. "Video games have turned martial arts into a fantasy. Pentium may have been inspired by my skills, yet many of the techniques in VK wouldn't work in the real world. But Bruce Lee's do."

My eye is drawn to the window and a Street Screen outside. I swear it'd been showing the VK logo with a picture of my face! But now there's only a vlogger talking about the riches he has made in Virtua.

"Am I boring you?" Sifu asks.

"No, of course not," I reply, waving away a fly buzzing over my food. "I just think I saw—"

Sifu catches the insect between his chopsticks, as fast as a scorpion. I am both amazed at his skill and a bit disgusted that he has used his chopsticks to catch a *fly*! But then he holds the crushed insect before my eyes. The wings are made of plastic, the body is a tiny microchip and the eyes are cameras.

Sifu frowns at me. "Someone is watching you."

The streets are clogged with traffic as I hurry back to the Power Inc. offices. I take a holo-picture of the fly in my hand while I walk and send it to Cookie with a message:

Been bugged. What do you make of this?

A minute later my cell earpiece rings and I hear Cookie's voice. "It's a high-grade military spy bug," she tells me. "But I don't understand why anyone would want to spy on *you.*"

"Nor do I," I reply.

"How long do you think it's been following you?" Cookie asks me.

A chill creeps across my skin. "At least since yesterday," I tell her. "I remember swatting a fly during training. Then in the street I had this *feeling* I was being watched. At first I thought it was a cleaner droid, then Stick and his gang. But it must have been this bug!"

"I'll examine it as soon as you're back," Cookie says. "I might be able to trace its signal and identify the bug's owner. Whatever, you need ... careful ... don't ..."

"Cookie?" I tap my earpiece but all I get is static. I've lost the connection.

My heart hammers in my chest as I dash down the road. I look around nervously. The few people on the street ignore me. Those in Auto-Taxis have their eyes on their cell-screens. No one is paying me any attention. But I still feel my every move is being watched.

A blast of horns and pounding drums sounds from a Street Screen ahead. My Ad Blocker must have failed. Then I recognise the music – it's the theme tune for VK! I look up and see Vince's tanned face on the screen, all shiny teeth and perfect skin. I skid to a stop. My blood runs cold at the sight of him.

"VK IS BACK!" Vince declares with pride. "AND IT'S NO LONGER JUST A GAME!"

This time I *know* I'm not imagining him. This is no glitch. Other people have looked up too.

"THE MOST REALISTIC FIGHTING GAME EVER HITS THE STREETS!" Vince says. "HUNT! FIGHT! KILL ... FOR REAL!"

The VK horns and drums blare out. Then the screen switches to a different advert and

the music disappears. My Ad Blocker seems
to be working again, and the city falls into a
strange silence. I can hear the thrum of traffic
and the light drizzle of rain like a distant wave.
The pounding of my blood grows loud in my
ears.

Then I start running. Running for my life.

My feet splash in puddles as I dart across
the street and around a corner. But a huge
gunmetal robot blocks my path. This is no
traffic bot or blue and white robocop. It looks
more like a military borg, with its pulse-rifle
and armour plating. A human face is projected
on its visor.

"Target located," the borg says, and aims its
rifle at me.

I dive behind an Auto-Taxi. The borg's laser pulse blows the roof off. Before a second shot blasts the taxi to pieces, I make a run for it, zig-zagging between the traffic. Cutting across the next road, I duck into a dark alley and find a dumpster. I hide in its shadow, hoping to lose the borg. But I soon hear the metal *clang* of its feet. As the borg enters the alleyway, I press myself further into the darkness and hold my breath.

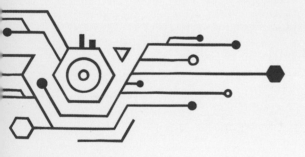

The borg draws closer and closer. Its shadow looms large on the alley wall. I hear a high-pitched *hum* as the borg powers up its pulse-rifle. There is nowhere for me to run. I'd be blasted into pulp on my first step!

Then I notice a waft of hot air on my legs and a foul smell drifts up from the ground. I look down – beneath my feet is a metal sewer grate. With no other option, I drop to my knees and wrench it open. The rusted metal screeches, giving away my location to the borg. It stomps towards my hiding place.

I dive into
the sewer just as
the borg flings the
dumpster aside. The
heavy grate crashes
back down and I scurry
along the tunnel like a spooked rat. Behind
me, the borg tears off the grate like tinfoil.
The sewer entrance is too small for it to follow
me ... but not for its rifle!

I throw myself to the slimy floor as a white
bolt of light shoots towards me. The laser
streaks over my head, the blast scorching
my skin and blowing a hole in the brickwork.
Before the borg can fire again, I scramble to my
feet and rush round a bend.

The sewer is dark and dirty. I crawl along,
my head bumping and my elbows scraping in
the tight space. Rats scurry away as my feet
splosh in the stinking stream. After several
minutes of cramped shuffling, I come to

another grate. I push it aside, climb out onto a side street and try my best to wipe the muck from my clothes.

Suddenly my cell bursts into life. *"Scott, are you there?"* Cookie shouts in my earpiece.

"Yes," I reply. "I've just been attacked by some laser-shooting robot!"

"Java and the others are looking for you," Cookie says. "We were worried when we lost contact. I'll ping them your location."

"Don't worry, I'm on my way—"

I'm cut off as a metal hand grabs me and slams me against a wall. Another borg is standing over me, a different face projected onto its visor – fat with bulging eyes and a leering grin.

"Prepare to be terminated!" the borg says.

I try to run, but it smashes me in the chest and I collapse to the ground. My ribs bruised, I can hardly breathe. I lie helpless, unable to move as the borg raises both fists to crush me with a hammer-blow. But at the top of its swing, the borg freezes. Its face on the visor blinks out and all the power drains from the machine.

"I honestly didn't think … that would work!" Java says, still panting from her run to save me. She holds up her EMP gun. "These weapons are made to knock out a Wasp drone, not a giant robot!"

Spam and Pac-Man arrive and help me to my feet.

"*Gross!* You smell like a toilet!" Spam says, holding his nose. He glances at my trousers. "Did you—"

"NO!" I protest. "I had to use the sewers to escape one of those things!"

"What the hell is it anyway?" Pac-Man asks as he eyes the dead droid.

Java inspects the metal casing of the de-powered borg. "Looks like it's designed for combat. It must be military."

Spam frowns. "What would an army bot be doing in the city?"

"Trying to kill *me* it seems," I reply.

"But who would want to kill you?" Pac-Man asks.

Spam's jaw drops open and he points up to a Street Screen. "I guess ... *everyone!*"

A screen the size of a football pitch is showing *my* face and the words:

VK3
NO.1 TARGET
BOUNTY – 10 MILLION CREDITS!

My body is frozen to the spot in shock. "Vince said VK is no longer just a game," I murmur.

Spam looks at me. "Do you mean VK is being played for *real?*"

I nod. "I told you Vince was back," I say. "The city has become his hunting ground and *I'm* the prey!"

Java's brow creases in thought. "If that's the case," she says, "then these robots must work like our online avatars. They must be controlled remotely by gamers."

"So there are *more* of them?" Spam asks.

"At least one more," I reply.

Pac-Man's eyes widen as he directs our attention to the Street Screen again. "Don't think Scott gets all the glory," he says.

Java's face is being displayed, along with a 5 million bounty. Followed by images of Pac-Man, Cookie and Spam – all with rewards for a kill.

"*What?* Only 2 million credits!" Spam cries as his face flashes up. "Is that all I'm worth?"

"I'd be glad if I were you," I reply. "It'll mean fewer gamers hunting you."

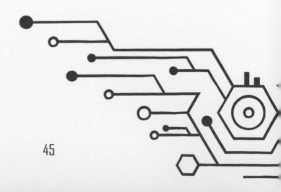

Horns begin blaring. This time it isn't the VK theme tune – the traffic on the main street has stopped. We step out onto the pavement to see what the problem is. Up ahead, two borgs have blocked the road. As soon as they spot us, they move in our direction.

"RUN!" I cry.

We sprint down the street, weaving between the traffic. The borgs follow us. At a crossroads we turn the corner but come face to face with two more borgs. One of them picks up an empty Auto-Taxi and hurls it at us. We dive aside as the taxi smashes into the pavement. The other borg blasts several rounds with its pulse-rifle and the taxi explodes in a ball of flames.

"This is no game!" Spam screams, shielding his head from the burning rubble. "This is madness!"

As the borgs close in on us from in front and behind, I shout to Java, "Use your EMP!"

"I can't!" she replies. "I used max power to stop the first one. The battery's dead."

"Then how are we supposed to fight back?" says Pac-Man. "In VK, at least we had weapons and Mods."

"We'll have to split up," says Java. "Divide their forces."

Nodding, Pac-Man and Spam rush across the road and down an alleyway. Java and I head in the opposite direction. Two borgs give chase.

We switch left, then right, trying to lose them. A blast from a pulse-rifle hits a neon sign over our heads. The huge sign explodes and we dive aside to avoid getting crushed. But Java goes one way and I leap the other. Now sheets of jagged glass and deadly sparks of electricity separate us.

"Meet you back at Power Inc.!" Java cries. She ducks down a side alley, a borg in hot pursuit.

The remaining borg with the pulse-rifle now takes aim at me. I flee as a laser blast vaporises a shop window. My heart pounding, I dart across a busy crossroads. An Auto-Taxi almost runs me over, but I keep going. Then I hear an almighty crash and glance back. The borg, in its rush to catch me, has mis-timed its crossing and collided with an industrial road-sweeper. The impact has destroyed both borg and sweeper. I run on, not risking another look back.

●

When I finally reach the Power Inc. building, I find Cookie waiting in reception, pacing back and forth. "What's going on?" she asks.

"Vince Power ... is back," I explain, trying to catch my breath. "He's launched VK3 ... and this version's no longer just a game ... it's real!"

I look around the glass reception area and ask, "Where are the others?"

Cookie gives me a nervous look. "They're not here yet."

I get a sinking sensation in my stomach and pray that my friends are safe. "OK, you wait for them," I say. "I'll go and see Pentium. He'll know what to do."

I take the hyper-lift up to the top floor. My mind is buzzing, unable to compute Vince's return from the dead. *How did he survive? How has he created a new Virtual Kombat? Where did he get the robots from?*

The lift doors ping open and I step into the penthouse office. Pentium is in his wheelchair, staring out of the huge floor-to-ceiling window at the city lit in neon below.

"Have you seen the Street Screens?" I ask as I hurry over to him.

"Of course I have," Pentium replies without turning round. "So ... how are you enjoying my new game?"

I stop in my tracks, unable to believe what I just heard. Then the pieces begin to fall into place.

Pentium's new game ...

Augmented reality …

The real world … only better!

His promise that I'd get first look.

Furious, I glare at Pentium. "*You* launched VK3!"

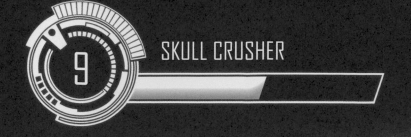

SKULL CRUSHER

Anger and confusion rise up in me as I charge over to Pentium. "Why would you do such a thing?" I ask him. "Why target me and the others?"

Pentium doesn't answer. I spin his wheelchair round to confront him. His mouth is taped over, his arms are bound to his chair and his eyes are wild with panic. I stare back in shock. *How could he have talked before?*

Then I hear a laugh, low and cruel, from the dark east wing of the office.

"My brother is a bit tied up at the moment," a smooth voice identical to Pentium's says.

I flinch with horror as a mechanical man strides out of the shadows. His body is encased in red steel. His arms and legs are super-sized robotic limbs. His face is half masked with circuits  and scanners, and his skull is clear glass – his brain replaced with a pulsing cybernetic processor of microchips and human tissue.

"*Vince?*" I ask.

Pentium's brother gives me a cold metallic smile. "The new, enhanced Vince!" he replies.

I look him up and down. "*What* are you?"

"The next evolution of man!" he says proudly. "A cyborg."

I shake my head, stunned. "But how did you survive VK? You were trapped in an Infinity Drop."

Vince's unnatural grin widens. "The destruction of VK actually saved me," he explains. "As your virus corrupted the game's code, it corrupted the Infinity Drop too. A door opened to another level and I was able to escape. Mind you, I was pretty burned out by then. Left paralysed from the neck down, like my brother." Vince scowls at Pentium. "But my Analysts did a fine job of rebuilding me from my instructions, don't you think?"

Vince admires his mutant form in the reflection of the window.

"I guess beauty really is in the eye of the beholder!" I say. To me, the once handsome

Vince Power is now a Frankenstein of flesh and machine.

Vince glares at me, then strides over to his brother, tied up in his wheelchair. "I must admit, I was surprised to discover Pentium was behind the VK virus. I thought he was still in a coma. Besides, he was the original creator of VK – I don't understand why he'd want to destroy it!" Vince looks over at me. "Talking of which, do you remember the VK avatar called Destroy?"

I nod slowly. Destroy was one of VK's star players – a heavyweight boxer who once almost killed me in the game.

"I rather liked his trademark move," Vince says with a smirk. "What was it called again?"

"The Skull Crusher," I reply.

"Ah, yes! That's it," Vince says. "I've always wondered what that move would be like in real life ..."

He places his metal fists on either side of Pentium's head, whose wild eyes bulge in terror. Then Vince slams his hands together. There's a sickening crunch that reminds me of the coffee cup exploding and I have to put my hand over my mouth to stop myself vomiting.

Vince shakes the bloody remains of his dead brother's head from his robotic hands. "Mmm, that was a bit messy!"

"You're insane!" I gasp.

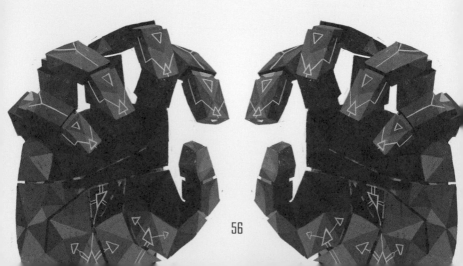

Vince swivels towards me. "I'll take that as a compliment."

I back away. "So are you going to kill me too?"

Vince shakes his glass-domed head. "No, that would spoil the game." He presses an icon on his mechanical arm and a hidden door slides open to reveal two borgs. "But these gamers might want to!"

The two borgs stride into the office. I'm like David against a pair of Goliaths – there's hardly any chance I'll defeat the borgs. I have no weapons. I'm half their size. And I am just flesh and blood against their steel and oil.

As they advance towards me, Vince says, "Do *try* to put up some sort of a fight, Scott! I've invested a lot of time and money in VK3. The borgs themselves cost a fortune! I literally had to buy a whole battalion from the military."

I picture several hundred borgs hunting the city for me and my friends, and any hopes

I had of survival fade. I turn to Vince. "You reprogrammed VK and bought a robot army just for *revenge*?"

"No, of course not," Vince replies with a laugh. "I also did it for entertainment *and* profit. Players are paying top dollar to control these borgs and get a chance to kill the kid that brought down their favourite game."

The digital faces on the visors glower with hatred at me.

"And your death makes for great entertainment!" Vince points to a massive Street Screen on the city skyline. A live video stream is playing. I can see myself in the office, the two borgs towering over me. "The world is watching, Scott!" Vince says. "Give them a wave."

The two borgs actually do wave to the hidden camera. In that moment of distraction, I make a run for the lift. But one of them grabs

me by the neck and flings
me across the office.
I crash into the wall.
The other borg picks up
Pentium's holo-desk to
crush me with it.

Scrambling to my feet, I rush over to
Pentium's lab, dive inside and lock the door
behind me. Desperate, I look around for
another exit and spot the exo-suit on its stand.

Without a second thought, I climb into
it. The black metal plates adjust to my body,
wrapping me in a skin of armour. The helmet
slides on and the visor lights up. I feel a
sharp jolt in my neck and suddenly the suit
becomes part of me. I lift my arm slowly. The
movement is exaggerated and I knock a lab
bench over like it's made of cardboard.

*Pentium's techs can't have fine-tuned the
strength settings yet!*

A moment later the lab door is kicked in and the two borgs enter. Their digital faces show surprise when they see me cocooned in a bitanium suit. I pray that Pentium was telling the truth when he said his exo-suit made him a superman and charge head first at the two borgs. Like a hyper-train, I collide full-force with them and they're thrown backwards like a child's toy, despite their greater size.

As I re-enter the office, Vince stares at my exo-suit with astonishment and even a touch of envy. "Well, my brother has certainly been busy!" Vince says, and claps with his huge metal hands. "Scott, this is even better than I could've planned – a clash of cyborgs!"

The two borgs are back on their feet in fighting stances, as if they were playing in VK. I raise my fists to defend myself. But being new to the suit, my movements are jerky. I have power but not full control yet. The first borg fires off a side-kick and I try to block it.

But I'm too slow and the powerful kick knocks me off my feet. I stumble backwards and crash into the office window. The glass shatters and I tumble out. The building flashes past as I plummet to the ground far below ...

"Scott?" Cookie cries. I open my eyes and she's gazing down at me with concern. "Is that you in there? Are you OK?"

Opening my visor, I slowly sit up, feeling dazed. The tarmac around me is rubble. I look up the sheer glass side of the Power Inc. building and realise I fell more than thirty storeys. Yet my body is in one piece. So too is the bitanium armour protecting me. Pentium was right about its strength. The exo-suit absorbed the impact without a scratch.

"I'm fine," I reply, and stand with the help of my suit. "Where are the others? Are they here yet?"

Cookie shakes her head. "The borgs stopped them, so they made for the old VKR base instead. It's off the grid – they're safe."

"Safe sounds good," I reply. "Let's join them."

"What happened up there?" Cookie asks as we cross the road and head for the base. "Is Pentium all right?"

The hyper-lift doors open in Power Inc.'s reception area and the two borgs emerge, on the hunt.

"No time to explain," I say, breaking into a sprint. "We need to get out of here fast!"

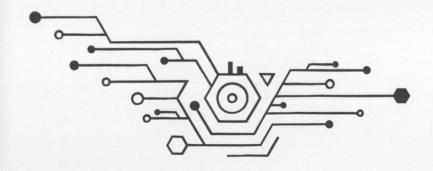

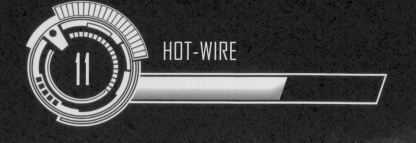
We take a disused stairwell down to a former subway station – the old VKR base. The foyer is dark and silent, the escalators and ticket machines out of order for years.

Java steps out from the shadows with her EMP gun raised. "What the hell, Cookie? You led a borg here!"

Cookie holds her hands up. "It's only Scott."

I flip back my visor and Java lowers her gun with a sigh. "Good thing too," she says. "This gun has no juice anyway!"

"What are you wearing?" Pac-Man asks me as he appears in the foyer with Spam.

"Pentium's exo-suit," I reply.

Spam stares at me wide-eyed behind his glasses. "You look like Pac-Man after a workout!"

I disconnect the electrodes and step out of the suit. "It might be our only defence against these borgs," I reply.

"Then we need more suits," Java says.

"Pentium only made this one as far as I'm aware," Cookie replies.

"Where is Pentium?" asks Spam.

I bow my head, grief suddenly weighing me down. "Vince killed him. He used Destroy's

Skull Crusher move to ..." I can't go on – the memory of Pentium's murder is too much to bear.

The shock news stuns everyone into silence. Tears run freely from Cookie's eyes. Java clenches her fists in fury, while Pac-Man punches a ticket machine. Spam just looks lost, unable to take in our mentor's death.

Pac-Man finally steps away from the battered ticket machine and says, "I don't know about you, but I always feel better after food."

We trail mournfully into the subway's staff canteen. We order chicken noodles from an auto-vending machine and slump down at a long metal table. As we eat, I update my friends about Vince and his robot army of borgs.

"I can't believe Vince is still alive," Java growls. She is so angry that she breaks her chopsticks in half.

"If you can call him *alive*," I reply. "Vince is a cyborg. Part man, part machine. I think his brain was corrupted by the virus too – he's insane."

"Insane or not, if Vince is super-human, how are we going to stop him? Or his borgs?" Cookie asks.

"We don't," Spam says. "We simply hide. Here, where it's safe."

Pac-Man looks at him, unsure. "You think the borgs won't hunt us down in this subway?"

"No one knows of this place except us," Spam replies. "And if we don't play the game, there is no game."

"What do you mean?" Java asks.

"If the players lose interest in the game, VK3 becomes obsolete," Spam explains. "No players, no borgs, no battle. Vince loses!"

Cookie nods to agree. But Java shakes her head. "That could take days, perhaps weeks!" she argues. "We don't have the supplies to last that long."

"I agree," Pac-Man says. "Besides, as soon as we poke our heads above ground, what's to stop Vince relaunching the game?"

Spam sighs heavily and prods at his noodles.

"Even if we did stay here, Spam," I say, trying to console him, "do you *really* think Vince will give up that easily? That he'll just let us hide?"

Spam looks at me. "Then what do you suggest?"

"We need more EMP guns," I reply. "They're the best way to stop these borgs."

"There's one small problem with that plan," Java says as she cradles her gun in her hand. "We don't have any more EMPs, and this one is only good for a single charge at a time. I don't like our odds of one EMP against several hundred robots!"

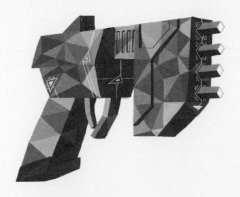

"I can try to make more EMPs," Cookie offers, "but it'll take time – and more battery packs."

"There's a whole load of them at the Power Inc. offices," Pac-Man says.

Spam smiles thinly. "And how are we going to get *into* the offices now that Vince is back in charge? He has an army of borgs at his disposal. We'd be dead before we even reached reception."

We fall silent, all trying to think of a solution. Then Java says, "We cut the head off the snake, so to speak. No Vince, no VK."

"What, we *kill* Vince?" The idea makes me feel uneasy. I'm no murderer.

"From what you say, he's barely alive anyway," Java replies.

"Java's right," Pac-Man says. "It's either him or us."

"But he's a super-powered cyborg – how do we fight that?" Spam asks. "Scott is the only one with an exo-suit."

I'm stumped for an answer. Even with my exo-suit, it would be suicidal for me to go on a one-man mission against a battalion of military borgs and an insane cyborg. Then Cookie says quietly, "We could hot-wire some of the VK borgs."

I frown at her. "How?"

"Vince's borgs are controlled remotely by online gamers," Cookie explains. "We have our old PlayPods here. If I can connect one to a borg, then we can take control of it, just like a VK avatar."

"Genius idea!" Pac-Man shouts, punching the air. "We could recruit our own army."

"And where do we get these borgs from exactly?" Spam asks.

"What about that one I zapped in the alley?" Java says.

Cookie nods. "We should only need to replace its circuit-breaker and over-ride its wireless connection."

"Then let's do it," I say, rising to my feet.

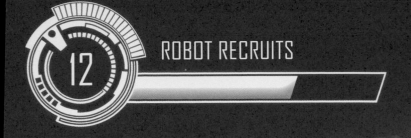

Less than an hour later, I stand guard at the entrance to the alley as Java climbs on top of the red borg. She opens a small panel in the back of its metal head.

"First, connect the over-ride chip," Cookie instructs on our cell earpieces. "Then insert the new circuit-breaker."

Java looks at me in my exo-suit. "Be ready to protect me in case this borg goes rogue," she says.

I nod, my muscles tense. As soon as the chip and breaker are in, the borg powers up.

Java leaps away. For a second or two, the borg does nothing. Then it pivots towards us and raises its metal fists. Java ducks behind me and draws her EMP gun.

"Cookie!" I call into my cell. "The over-ride chip isn't working!"

All of a sudden the borg starts to dance and I hear Pac-Man's laugh over the borg's speakers.

"Got you, bud!" he says. His rugged face appears on the visor screen. "I'm *all* in control." The borg finishes its dance with a bow.

"You zaphead, Pac-Man!" Java snaps, pocketing her gun. "I almost fried the borg again."

"Chill," Pac-Man replies. "Cookie's plan worked."

"One borg doesn't make an army," Spam reminds us over our cells.

"Then let's find some more recruits!" I say.

We head out into the street, me and the borg on either side of Java like two metal bodyguards. It's not long before we run into a unit of four VK borgs.

"So how do we recruit them, exactly?" Pac-Man asks as they advance on us.

"Ask nicely?" Java suggests.

One of the borgs powers up a pulse-rifle and another flashes a laser sword.

"I don't think nice will work," I say. "We need to disable them."

As the borg with the laser sword rushes forward to slice Java in two, she fires off her EMP gun. The borg loses power and stops mid-swing. But now the EMP charge has gone, Java's gun is useless against the other robots. They thunder towards us and Pac-Man moves his borg to protect Java. He drives a great steel fist into the lead borg's chest, smashing it backwards into a vacant shop. The building collapses on top of it.

"Oops!" Pac-Man says. "My borg is a bit stronger than I thought."

The third borg aims its pulse-rifle at me, no doubt hoping for the 10 million bounty. I may be smaller, but I'm more agile now my body has adapted to the exo-suit. I dart forwards, dodging the laser shot. Then I knock the weapon from the borg's grasp and turn the rifle on it. With a single blast, I take out the borg's power unit. It drops to the ground, a pile of junk metal.

"Try not to destroy *all* the recruits!" Cookie pleads in my ear.

"Sorry," I say, and discard the rifle. "It's a bit hard when they're out to kill us!"

Java cries for help as the fourth and final borg grabs her. Without an exo-suit, she'll be crushed like an ant. I run over and knock the borg to the ground. Pac-Man leaps on top as I try to prise open its steel claws. But the robot is incredibly strong. Java starts screaming. I strain with all my might. My exo-suit boosts my strength and I'm able to free Java from the borg's deadly grip.

As she gasps with pain, Java takes an over-ride chip from her pocket. "Hold the borg still!" she orders.

Together Pac-Man and I manage to pin it down and Java inserts the chip. The borg stops struggling and a second later Spam's face pops up on the visor screen.

"Boy, that's one ugly borg!" Pac-Man teases Spam.

"At least it's now *our* borg," I say as Spam sticks out a digital tongue at us.

"We have our army," Java says as we stand in the subway foyer admiring the line-up of my black exo-suit and the three recruited borgs.

"Woo-hoo, we're saved!" Spam says, his tone sarcastic. "Four robots against hundreds of killer borgs! A sure victory!"

"We don't have to win a war, just one battle," I remind him.

"Think of it like a video game," Java says. "Our objective is to raid the Power Inc. offices. First we'll need to evade and overcome the borg guards, then fight our way up to the penthouse and finally take down the big boss."

"Sounds like a cool game," Spam says sarcastically. "But this is for *real*. How many lives do we get?"

Java shrugs. "I suppose as many borgs as we can recruit."

Cookie nods. "Unlike VK2, you shouldn't die if your borg dies. The neural link is just mechanical."

"That's reassuring," says Spam with a forced smile.

Pac-Man glances at me. "We should capture a borg for you too, Scott. No point in risking your life in the exo-suit."

I know Pac-Man is right, but I've become quite attached to my new super-suit. In fact, without it I feel like I'm missing a limb. I wonder if the neuro-connection is developing a permanent link with my mind – a co-dependency between me and the suit.

"I agree," Java says. "Tomorrow we should try to recruit two more borgs. One for Scott and one for Cookie. Then we launch our assault."

"So what's the plan for that?" Spam asks.

We head to the console room that houses the PlayPods. Cookie pulls up a digital map of the Power Inc. offices on her console screen. "We must assume Vince will be in his penthouse office," she begins. "We approach the building in two units – one to the front entrance, one to the rear. I'm hoping our recruited borgs can blend in with the other borgs on the streets. If we encounter resistance, then ..."

As Cookie outlines her plan, I'm distracted by the sound of buzzing. At first I think it's just the hum of the old strip light. Then I start to wonder if it's another spy-fly and glance around nervously. But the sound grows louder.

Java notices it too and frowns. "What's that noise?"

"It's coming from the foyer," Spam says.

"Perhaps it's one of the borgs powering down?" Pac-Man suggests.

I shake my head. The buzz is worryingly familiar, but I can't quite place it. I step out of the console room and back into the foyer. Apart from the three borgs and my exo-suit, the subway is deserted. But the buzzing echoes across the station, growing ever louder like an approaching train.

Then an insect-like drone, yellow and black, flies out of the stairwell. More follow it.

"*Wasps!*" I gasp, finally recognising the sound. The others hear my warning and rush from the console room. On instinct, I leap into my exo-suit and the metal plates wrap round me in a protective second skin.

"How did they find us?" Spam cries as a Wasp drone zips our way, its Stinger ready to strike.

"We can worry about that later," Java replies. "For now, we get out of here!"

As the swarm of yellow and black drones floods the foyer, we rush for the escalators and head down to the lower tunnels. The angry buzz chases us all the way onto the platforms.

"Get to the exit!" Java shouts. Off the tunnels is a gated passage – an emergency escape route. We jump down onto the tracks, sprinting for our lives. But a Stinger hits Cookie and she goes down.

"No!" I cry, turning back to help her. The Wasp hovers over her shuddering body. I bat it away with my steel arm, but more and more drones pour onto the platform. Cookie is stung again and again. I'm protected by my suit, yet the swarm still drives me back.

"Come on!" Java yells, waiting by the gate. The others are safely in the passage.

My suit starts to spark, the Wasps' electro-darts overpowering the system. Cookie is no longer moving and I realise it's too late to save her. I have no choice – I flee down the tunnel, leaving her behind.

We sit in a huddle in Sifu's martial arts hall. With our base over-run by Wasps and Pentium's office now in Vince's hands, it's the only place we could think of going. Our plan is in tatters and our hearts broken by another loss.

Spam sobs into his hands. "Cookie ... she can't be ... she can't be ... *dead*!"

"No one could survive that many stings," Java says flatly.

"But why did *she* have to die?" Pac-Man spits with bitterness. "I'd gladly give my life for hers!"

"Cookie's death has meant you have all lived," Sifu says. He lights a candle upon a small Buddhist shrine and begins to pray in her memory.

I stare in silent fury out of a window at a Street Screen. Cookie's face is being shown with the words:

TARGET DEAD
BOUNTY CLAIMED – 3 MILLION CREDITS!
4 TARGETS REMAINING

Vince is *celebrating* Cookie's death. Using it to promote VK3. Spurring the gamers to hunt down the rest of us for more bounties. I punch the training dummy with my armoured fist, shattering its wooden frame. Then I lash out at the punchbag and it explodes in a cloud of stuffing.

"Save your energy for the borgs," Java tells me. "You're our only defence now!"

On cue, a gunmetal borg strides into the hall. I charge at it, all my anger and rage coming out in a barrage of punches and kicks. My exo-suit inflicts so much damage that I'm like a wrecking ball. The borg stands no chance and is torn to pieces. I stand over the remains of it, trembling.

"That's for Cookie, you useless hunk of metal!" I shout.

My friends stare at me, shocked by my violence and fury.

Then Java asks, "How did that borg find us so fast?"

I shrug. "Remember that spy-fly? Vince knows about this location. He must have tipped off the VK players."

Pac-Man gets to his feet. "We should leave then. Find somewhere else to hide."

"Wait!" Java says. "That still doesn't explain how the Wasps found our base? *No one* knew that location, apart from us."

"Another spy-fly?" Spam suggests.

"Maybe … but I think the spy is among us." Java turns towards Sifu, who is still kneeling by the shrine.

"Not Sifu?" I exclaim. "He's a friend of Pentium's."

Java's eyes narrow. "But who's to say he isn't a friend of Vince's too? I mean, what do we *really* know about our teacher?"

Sifu continues to pray, seeming not to have heard Java's accusation.

"Why would Sifu betray us?" Pac-Man asks.

"To claim the bounties, of course," Java replies. "He'd be rich beyond his dreams."

"That's crazy!" I say. "Sifu doesn't even know the location of our base. So how could *he* be to blame?"

"Then who is the traitor, Scott?" Java demands. "Sifu isn't denying it."

Sifu turns from his prayers. "The question isn't whether I deny it or not," he says softly. "But whether *you* would believe me?"

Java shakes her head in dismay. "I don't know what to believe any more."

"Perhaps the traitor doesn't know they're a traitor," Spam suggests.

"What do you mean?" I ask.

Spam points at me. "Maybe your exo-suit is to blame? It could have a locating device."

I study my suit uneasily, then disconnect and step out. "You think so?" I ask.

Spam pulls out a mobile gaming unit from his pocket and loads a monitor app. He scans the suit, but the app stays green. "No signals detected," he says, frowning. But as he moves towards me, the app begins to buzz. Spam sweeps the device over my body. The app turns red when it passes over my right arm.

"It's just my Ad Blocker," I say.

But Spam gives me a dark look. "That's no Ad Blocker!"

I stare with horror at the tiny bump on my arm. All along the traitor was *me*. I led the Wasps to our base. I put the team in danger. *I* am the reason Cookie is dead.

"*Pentium* implanted a tracker in you?" Pac-Man gasps.

I slowly shake my head. "The tech who brought the Ad Blocker. He must have been working for Vince!"

Java inspects the buried chip. "We need to get it out."

"How?" I ask.

"I can *blaze* it out
for you," a voice snarls
behind me. We spin
round to find Stick and
his gang have crept
into the hall.

"Thanks for your offer of help,
Stick," I reply with a thin smile, "but
we don't have time for this. We're
being hunted by Vince and his borgs—"

"I know," Stick says. "You're worth 10
million credits, Scott, and it's time to collect
my prize!"

Stick powers up a new Blazer. But as he
advances on me, the doors to the hall implode
and two borgs march in.

"Looks like you've got some competition!"
Spam says.

The borgs wade past Stick's gang, batting them aside like human skittles. In the chaos, Stick lunges at me. Without thinking, I leap into the air and strike back with a spinning hook-kick. Thanks to my extra training, I don't mis-judge the jump this time and my foot connects with Stick's head. He goes down like a pile of bricks, his Blazer clattering across the floor.

"Told you practice makes perfect!" Sifu says. Armed with a steel bo staff, he attacks the nearest borg. He jabs at its sensors and cameras, driving the borg back. Pac-Man and Spam grab a pair of bladed spears from the weapons wall and try to fend off the other borg.

Java snatches up Stick's Blazer and pulls me behind a pillar. "This'll hurt!" she warns.

Before I can protest, Java stabs the Blazer's laser tip into my flesh. I scream as she cuts out the tracker and then seals the wound with the flat side of the blade. "Wait here!" she orders, the tiny chip in her hand.

With tears of pain in my eyes, I clasp my wounded arm to my chest. All I can hear are the injured cries of Stick's gang and the clang of metal as Sifu, Pac-Man and Spam battle the borgs. I peer round the pillar and spot Java helping a dazed Stick sit up. He appears to be choking. Meanwhile Pac-Man and Spam have been backed into a corner by their borg. Realising they need my help, I dart over to the exo-suit and clamber in. As soon as the electrodes connect, a pain blocker kicks in and the agony in my arm fades.

Stick sees me in my suit and flees the hall. I stride over to Pac-Man and Spam, ready to do battle with the borgs, but they retreat into the street too.

"What ... just happened there?" Spam asks, panting heavily from the fight.

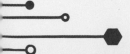

Pac-Man shrugs. "No idea. Perhaps Scott scared them off?"

Sifu hobbles over with Java. I glare at her. "Why were you helping Stick when the others were in trouble?" I demand.

"I didn't help him," Java replies. She gives me a guilty smile. "I made him swallow the tracker."

"You did *what?*" I cry.

"He's our decoy," Java explains.

"That's why the two borgs left!" Pac-Man laughs. "The gamers were chasing the target to get their bounty."

"But you've given Stick a death sentence," I say.

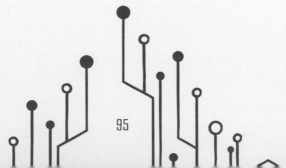

"Maybe," Java replies. "But he'll get rid of the tracker *naturally* in a day or so – if he can last that long."

"And then what?" Spam asks. "The borgs will be back on the hunt for *us*. We don't have a base. We can't stay here. We don't have PlayPods or even our recruited borgs. Apart from Scott's exo-suit, we're defenceless."

"Defeat is not defeat unless accepted as a reality in your own mind," Sifu says, leaning on his staff.

"Nice words, Sifu," Java replies, "but I'm afraid *that* is our reality."

She points to the Street Screen outside the hall. A VK3 advert declares:

No safe place to hide!

Cold and wet from the constant drizzle of acid rain, we walk in silence. Just the *clink* of Sifu's staff echoing down the back streets as we search the mega-city for a safe haven. But every Street Screen reminds us that there is nowhere we can hide. We can only run.

As we turn a corner, Java stops dead in her tracks.

I tense, expecting a unit of borgs. But there's just an abandoned VK Selector Truck in an otherwise empty parking area. "What's up?" I ask.

"Nothing," Java replies, "but I think we've found the solution to our problem."

"What? We *drive* out of the city?" Spam asks.

Java shakes her head. "No, we're back to our original plan."

"Of course!" I smile. "The truck's a mobile VK game station!"

Java nods. "The truck has PlayPods. We can connect them to our borg recruits." She turns to Spam. "How are your hacking skills?"

"I'm no Cookie ..." he says, the thought of her triggering a sad look on his face.

"But you worked with Cookie on the VK virus," Pac-Man reminds him. "You must know a thing or two."

Spam shrugs. "I'll give it a go."

We break into the truck and power it up. Spam seats himself at the console, stares at the log-in prompt, then begins to type. The rest of us sit around in tense silence, watching as Auto-Taxis and cleaner droids pass by. Thankfully no borgs or Wasps appear. But the VK updates on the Street Screens show them hunting the city for us, following Stick's tracker. Still I feel nervous. I don't like being so exposed on the street.

"How are you doing, Spam?" I ask after an hour has passed.

Spam leans back in his chair, rubbing his eyes. "I wish Cookie was here," he sighs.

"Keep going," I say. "I *know* you can do it."

Yet another hour goes by. A Wasp passes overhead and I'm worried we've been spotted. Then Spam shouts, "Bingo! Connected. Who wants to test it out?"

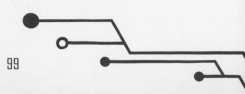

Both Java and Pac-Man leap into PlayPods and the hoodies slide down. Spam opens the link and their bodies begin to twitch – a sure sign they're controlling their borg avatars.

"It's working!" Spam says with a grin.

"Well done!" I say, clapping Spam on the back. "Cookie would be proud."

As we wait, I hear the *clang* of borg feet heading our way. I raise my armoured fists, ready to defend my friends. Two gunmetal borgs round the corner. But rather than fight, they give a cheery wave. Their visors show Java and Pac-Man's scanned faces. I relax my guard.

Spam jumps into a PlayPod and retrieves his own borg.

"We still need a robot for Sifu," Java says as Spam disconnects and sits up in his pod.

"Then we'll just recruit one," Pac-Man says.

Spam shakes his head. "We don't have any over-ride chips. Cookie had them all."

I curse and kick over a dumpster. A cleaner droid appears and starts to tidy up the mess.

"An army is not always made up of warriors," Sifu says.

We all look at him, puzzled. Then he points to the cleaner droid.

Spam smiles to himself. "City-bots have lower levels of encryption. In theory, I could hack into their wireless modules without needing an over-ride chip." He sits back at the console and taps away on the keyboard. "Sifu, climb into a PlayPod."

With an uneasy look, Sifu settles into a pod and its hoody slides down over his wrinkled face. A second later, the droid outside stops cleaning. Then it zips around the parking area like a mini battering ram.

"How do you control this thing?" Sifu cries.

"Just think and it will follow your command," I instruct him.

As the droid stutters backwards and forwards, Spam explains, "So I've hacked into the city-bot network. We now have access to any service bot we want."

"But what good will they do?" Pac-Man asks. "They're not armed or armoured like a borg."

"True," Spam replies, "but we can use them like kamikaze pilots and inflict some serious damage – and we have an army of thousands at our disposal."

Java grins at me. "It's time to cut the head off the snake!" she says.

Suddenly there's a blare of horns and pounding drums. The black and red VK logo twirls on Street Screens across the city as a voice announces, *"Calling all Elite Gamers! Return to your pods! The final battle begins!"*

Like rats out of a sewer, children in VK kombat suits start appearing on the street. They walk as if in a trance, heading in one direction ... the Power Inc. offices.

"What's going on?" Sifu asks as we watch the children continue their slow march across the city.

"The missing Elite Gamers!" I gasp. "The VK theme is calling them back, like the Pied Piper led the rats."

"This *cannot* be good," Java says. "Vince must be recruiting for another borg army!"

Just when I think our luck can't get any worse, I spot the Wasp again. The drone is guiding a unit of ten borgs towards the parking area. "I guess Stick didn't last as long as we hoped," I say.

"Time to get out of here," Java says.

"But we can't leave the truck undefended!" Pac-Man reminds us.

"We don't have to," Spam replies. "The truck can come with us. I can remote drive it."

"*You* can drive?" Java asks.

Spam offers a nervous grin. "Well, I'm in pole position on Speed Racer. I'm sure it can't be much different."

He re-routes his PlayPod from his borg to the truck's auto-drive. The engine fires up and the truck pulls away. The unit of borgs begin to chase us. They seem to know that their targets are on board and those with pulse-rifles start firing at the moving vehicle.

"Protect the truck!" I shout.

Sifu's cleaner droid makes a suicidal dash at the lead borg chasing us. They crash head-on and the droid is destroyed. But its sacrifice has paid off. The borg's leg is crippled and it crumples to the ground.

"I think I'm getting the hang of this!" Sifu laughs as Spam links his pod to a fresh city-bot, which powers off on another kamikaze run.

I cling on to the rear of the speeding truck while Pac-Man's and Java's borgs run alongside it, fending off any chasing borg that gets too close. Spam hurtles through the city, jumping red lights and weaving the truck between Auto-Taxis. It screeches round a corner and enters the city's central square. But the borgs are hot on our tail.

Java's robot is taken down by a pulse-blast. She immediately switches to Spam's unused borg, but it's been left far behind in the lot. Pac-Man has to battle the borgs alone.

"Keep going!" I order Spam as I leap off to help Pac-Man.

"NO! Stay with the truck!" Java shouts. "If we lose a fight, our robots die. But if you lose, *you* die!"

"Don't worry, my suit will protect me," I reply. I know I'm taking a great risk, but I need to give my friends in the truck every chance of escape.

Side by side, I fight with Pac-Man against the borgs. I use my *tae kwon do* skills and my exo-suit's strength to rip out vital wiring from one borg, damage the circuits of another and throw a third borg into a nearby building. Pac-Man smashes and pounds everything in his path until a borg with a laser sword slices off his left arm. He's about to lose his head too, when a cleaner droid darts out of nowhere and collides with his attacker head-on.

"Good work, Sifu!" I shout as the VK borg crumples to the ground.

By now, Java's borg has caught up and is attacking from behind. Pac-Man picks up a pulse-rifle with his borg's one remaining arm and begins firing. Between us, we manage to destroy the final four borgs until none are left standing.

Pac-Man drops the pulse-rifle to high-five me. "We won the battle!" he yells.

"But not the war," Java says darkly. She detaches an arm from a fallen borg, connects it to Pac-Man's robot, then claims the laser sword for herself.

On the Street Screens overhead, a replay of the battle is being shown and I realise our victory is Vince's profit! Anger rises up in me. Vince wins *whatever* the result. The longer we survive, the more money he makes.

The replay switches to a live feed of our fleeing truck. Spam has been forced to turn back by a fresh unit of borgs. He's speeding across the empty square, heading for the north exit. But more borgs appear to block his escape route and the truck skids to a stop.

"We're surrounded!" Spam calls over our cells.

We race over to defend the truck. Two robots, a cleaner droid and an exo-suit against *hundreds* of VK borgs. My anger is replaced by despair. I realise we're doomed.

The VK borg army closes in on us, every paying gamer keen to claim the bounties for themselves. Our robots stand in a ragged circle around the truck – a feeble line of defence for those inside. I summon up what courage I have. My exo-suit gives me strength but not much hope.

Then the borgs come to a sudden stop. Silence descends over the square – even the Street Screens go quiet.

A red cyborg steps from the ranks. Its pearl-white smile is half masked by circuits and a skull of glass. Somehow I'm not surprised to see the fame-hungry Vince Power at the front line of this battle.

"The game is almost over!" Vince declares. "You've played well, Scott. In fact, you've survived far longer than I expected."

I glare at Vince. "Sorry to disappoint you."

"Disappoint me?" Vince laughs. "The ratings for VK3 are the best ever! My profits are sky high! Honestly, I don't want the game to end."

"Then let us go!" Java says fiercely.

Vince shakes his head and grins. "I still want my revenge."

"And I want mine for Cookie!" Pac-Man shouts. He raises his pulse-rifle at Vince.

But before Pac-Man can pull the trigger, the VK theme tune blasts out of Street Screens everywhere. The display switches to a live video stream of the square and the VK borgs come back to life.

"Claim your bounties, players!" Vince orders.

The gamers resume their attack. Pac-Man fires his pulse-rifle at Vince, but a borg gets in the way and takes the blast instead. Then we're on the defence, fighting at close range. Java's borg is swinging its laser sword. Pac-Man's shooting his pulse-rifle. Sifu makes another kamikaze run. I'm punching and kicking with all my skill and strength.

Two borgs bear down on me. But, in their determination to be the *first* to kill and claim the top bounty, they begin to fight among themselves. Borg blasts borg. Gamer turns against gamer.

"NO!" Vince shouts. "Destroy the target! *He's* the prize!"

But the two gamers seem unwilling to share the prize.

The chaotic attack gives me the advantage. With the enemy divided, I bring down the two borgs.

"We might just survive this!" I say as Pac-Man blasts one borg and Java beheads another with her laser sword.

"Don't speak too soon," Spam replies. "I can't connect to any more city-bots. They've *all* gone offline. Vince must be jamming the signal!"

In a surprise combined attack from three borgs, Pac-man is suddenly overpowered. Java goes to his rescue but is destroyed by a direct blast from a pulse-rifle. As her robot explodes, Java shouts over her cell, "Run, Scott! Get away while you can!"

The borgs must sense that their targets are unprotected – they surge towards the truck.

"No," I reply, picking up Pac-Man's weapon. "We fight together, to the end!"

I leap on top of the truck and start firing at the enemy. I am the last defence ... then my pulse-rifle runs out of ammo.

Game over. Vince has won.

We fought with warrior spirit, but it was not enough. The borgs are just a pulse blast away from claiming their prize.

I drop my empty weapon and stare at Vince. After all we fought for – all the risks we took, all the sacrifices we made – he has beaten us. Vince grins back at me, relishing his ultimate victory.

Then a distant rumble makes him look round. His shocked expression tells me this isn't anything *he* planned.

From atop the truck I can see a legion of city-bots marching towards the central square from every direction. Cleaner droids, traffic bots, road-sweepers, dock-loaders, scrap-crushers, Auto-Taxis ... even robocops. A mish-mash army of moving metal.

"What's happening out there?" Java calls from inside the truck.

"I've no idea," I reply. "But it looks like the city-bots have come to our rescue!"

Attacking Vince's VK army, the city-bots ram, strike and smash all in their path. Their vast numbers overcome the borgs' superior armour and firepower. Each time a VK borg blasts a cleaner droid, another city-bot takes its place until the VK borg runs out of ammo and is destroyed.

"Is this your doing, Spam?" I ask.

Spam pops his head out of the truck's skylight and gawps at the scene. "No ... but it might explain why all the city-bots are offline."

Like a tidal wave the bots flood the central square, forcing the VK borgs to fight for their survival. The bounties for us are all but forgotten.

With his army on the brink of defeat, Vince retreats. I jump down from the truck to chase him. Java is right. The only way to end VK is to end Vince Power.

Dashing through the carnage, I confront Vince's cyborg. "Game over," I tell him.

Vince snarls. "The game is only over when *I* say it's over."

With his great steel fist, Vince punches me in the gut. It hits me like a car crash and I fly backwards into a VK borg. Only my exo-suit saves me from being killed by the impact.

I leap up and charge at Vince, bombarding him with punches. But Vince blocks them all. His reactions are faster than humanly possible. He strikes back 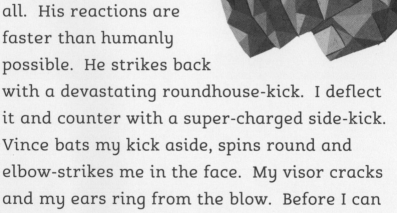 with a devastating roundhouse-kick. I deflect it and counter with a super-charged side-kick. Vince bats my kick aside, spins round and elbow-strikes me in the face. My visor cracks and my ears ring from the blow. Before I can recover, Vince hammer-fists my helmet and I drop to my knees.

Vince laughs. "You stand no chance against me, Scott. I've downloaded *every* martial art move from VK!"

In my daze, I recall what Sifu said: *Many of the techniques in VK wouldn't work in the real world. But Bruce Lee's do.*

Vince raises his fists over my head. "So let me finish what Destroy started ..." he goes on.

As he prepares to skull-crush me, I whisper into my cell, "Spam! Download every Bruce Lee file into my exo-suit!"

"What?" replies Spam.

"Just do it!" I say.

A moment later my suit's system pings with a new data file.

Vince gloats at me as he holds his great fists high. "I did warn you that VK is no longer just a game. The slogan 'So real it hurts' is even truer now ... and I promise you *this* will hurt."

As Vince's fists come down, I make a single thought command that sets off a chain reaction in my exo-suit. Having processed all Bruce Lee's techniques, the suit mimics his most lethal punch, creating a shockwave of energy that explodes into my armoured fist and smashes into Vince's cyborg. His metal exo-skeleton splits in the same way Sifu split the wooden post.

Vince staggers backwards and collapses to the ground, blue sparks streaking over him. "What … was that move?" he gasps, staring in horror at his fractured form.

"The one-inch punch," I reply.

He frowns at me. "There's no such punch in VK!"

"No," I reply, "but *I'm* not playing VK – and I never will again."

I pick up a discarded laser sword to end it once and for all. But before I can, a city-bot dock-loader grabs Vince and dumps him in a waiting scrap-crusher. Vince's broken figure is powerless to stop the crusher's jaws from closing on him. He lets out a distorted scream as his cyborg body is turned to scrap metal.

"Martial arts clearly *can* be an instant download!" Sifu admits as we all stand in the central square surrounded by piles of broken borgs and dead droids. "Scott, that was a perfect one-inch punch."

I laugh, amazed that my plan worked. "True martial arts is still a lifelong journey," I reply. "Without a master like you to show me the way, I'd never have known the move in the first place."

Java kicks away a stray piece of Vince's glass skull. "I guess the snake no longer has a head."

A cleaner droid scurries across to hoover up the piece of skull. Now the battle's over, the surviving city-bots appear to have returned to their normal functions.

Spam frowns. "But if Vince wasn't controlling the city-bots ... who was?"

I turn to Pac-Man, but he just shrugs.

"Perhaps *they* are your answer," Sifu says, and nods at a group of kids walking into the square. They all wear the black VK kombat suits of Elite Gamers.

A tall girl with the tag VIXEN on her suit waves to me. "Scott!" she shouts, jogging over. "What the hell's gone on here?"

I stare at my old friend from Vince's City Orphanage. "You *remember* me?"

Vixen nods. "Of course, we're Elite Gamers together. Except the last game was a bit odd ...

we could only be basic robots against an entire avatar army!" She looks around at the carnage, slowly realising what has just happened.

"Not only has your memory come back," I say, smiling. "You saved our lives!"

"I did?" Vixen replies, still confused.

"Yes! You and the others must have been controlling the city-bots that stopped the borgs," Spam explains.

Vixen frowns. "Oh, I thought that was just a game."

I shake my head. "VK is no longer just a game. In fact, it's no longer a game at all!"

We return to Power Inc. and head up to Pentium's penthouse office. As we step out of the lift, we're met by an astonishing sight. A

slim girl with a long fringe of brown hair is sitting behind the holo-desk.

"You're alive!" Spam cries, rushing over and hugging Cookie.

"How did *you* survive?" I ask as we cluster round the desk. I can see faint red lines of electrical scars still visible on her skin. "We saw you being stung to death!"

Cookie smiles and pats her grey jacket. "Electricity always seeks the path of least resistance," she explains. "When I build a PlayPod, I have to be careful of static shocks. So I wear carbon clothes. The carbon fibre conducts electricity and expels any charge. When the Wasps stung me, the electro-darts knocked me out, but most of their charge passed into the earth."

"Perhaps *I* should wear carbon clothes," Pac-Man says, "because it was a shock to see you die."

"So it was *you* who called the Elite Gamers back to their pods?" I ask Cookie.

She nods. "Once Vince thought I was dead, I was free to hack into the VK3 system. It was built on the same coding as VK2, so I didn't have any trouble accessing it. The Elite Gamers were still linked to their old PlayPods because of the virus we'd implanted. That's why they were in a trance."

"But their memories have come back now," Spam points out.

"Yes, their victory in VK has somehow freed them from the game and rebooted their brains," Cookie explains. "Like a hard drive reverting to its factory setting, I guess – their memories have been reset to the moment before they entered VK."

"So what now?" Pac-Man asks, gazing out of the office's broken window. The Street Screens are oddly silent and blank along the skyline of the neon mega-city.

"Time for a new game," Cookie says, and types a command into the holo-desk. "Something that will change the world … Pentium's augmented-reality project."

On every Street Screen, as far as the eye can see, a logo appears, bright and bold:

RL
RealLife

"What is it?" Spam asks.

"A game of social interaction," Cookie replies. "Players are rewarded for going out, making friends, visiting new places …"

"But a game *won't* change anything," Java argues.

"This one will," I say, and smile, remembering Pentium's words. "It's the real world ... only better."

Java was wrong.

The world did change.

For the better.

People are living in reality once more.

We are free to live our lives, the threat of VK and Vince Power no longer hanging over us.

So if you're reading this, remember ...

Life is not a game. It's your one chance to live!

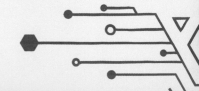

GAME
OVER?